GRAMBO

by Beth Navarro
illustrated by Betsy Hamilton

GRAMBO

Also available on
www.BeThereBedtimeStories.com
and www.MagicBlox.com

For Grandma Jean and Grandma H

—Beth Navarro

For Barbara, Geraldine and Rosella - my Grambos

—Betsy Hamilton

***Can you crack Grambo's secret code?

My grandma is not your average grandma. Sure, she has white hair, violet framed glasses, comfy, square shoes and bakes spectacular chocolate chip cookies.

Don't let that fool you.
My Grandma has SECRETS.

Upon her return from a trip
to Texas, I snuck in
and unzipped her suitcase.
She usually puts my souvenir
right on top. Nada!
So I poked around.
Peeking out from under her
flannel pajamas was a
cool new GPS device.

Why would Grandma need a
Global Positioning System?
Did Grandma pick up the
wrong suitcase? Maybe this
was my present! Cool!
But what does it say
here on the side...
government issued...?

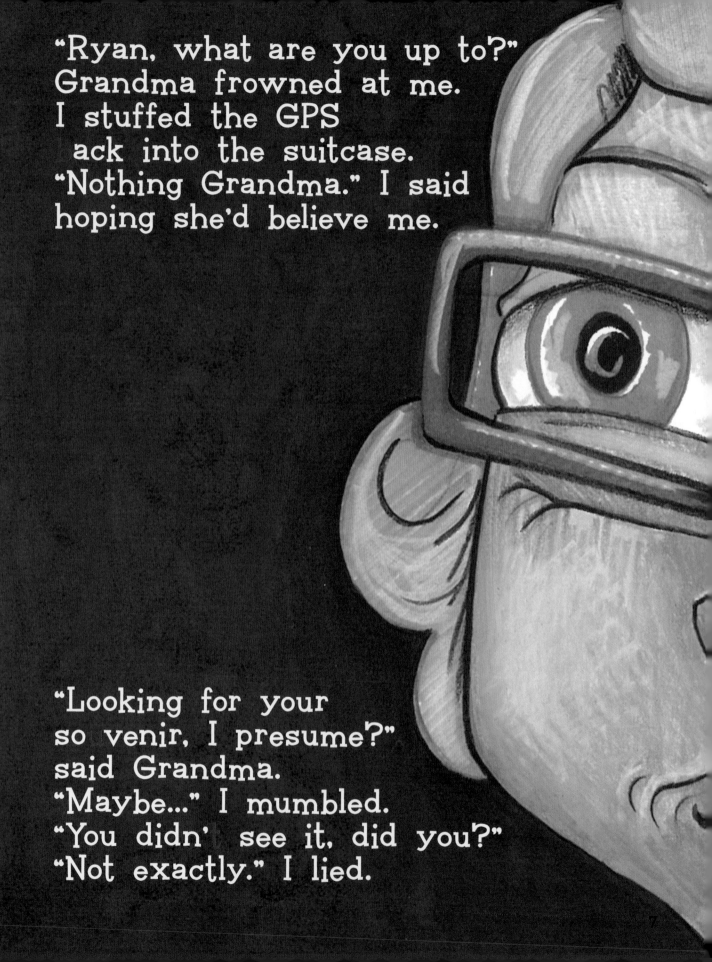

"Ryan, what are you up to?"
Grandma frowned at me.
I stuffed the GPS
 ack into the suitcase.
"Nothing Grandma." I said
hoping she'd believe me.

"Looking for your
so venir, I presume?"
said Grandma.
"Maybe..." I mumbled.
"You didn' see it, did you?"
"Not exactly." I lied.

Grandma rooted through her
suitcase. My heart thumped
so loud I thought it would
jump out of my chest.
Here it comes!
The best gift of all!

"Tada!" She flourished something:
not the GPS, but a...snow globe?
"Look Ryan! It's the Alamo.
Strange, it's snowing, but
I thought you'd like it."

"Uh, thanks." I said baffled.
When did Grandma learn
how to use a GPS?

Texas held the answer to Grandma's secret. So, the next time Grandma took a quick trip to Texas, I did what any curious grandson would do. I stowed away.

"Mom! I'm going to Frankie's house!" I fibbed. I hid under a blanket in the backseat of Dad's car, before he drove her to the airport. I followed her inside.

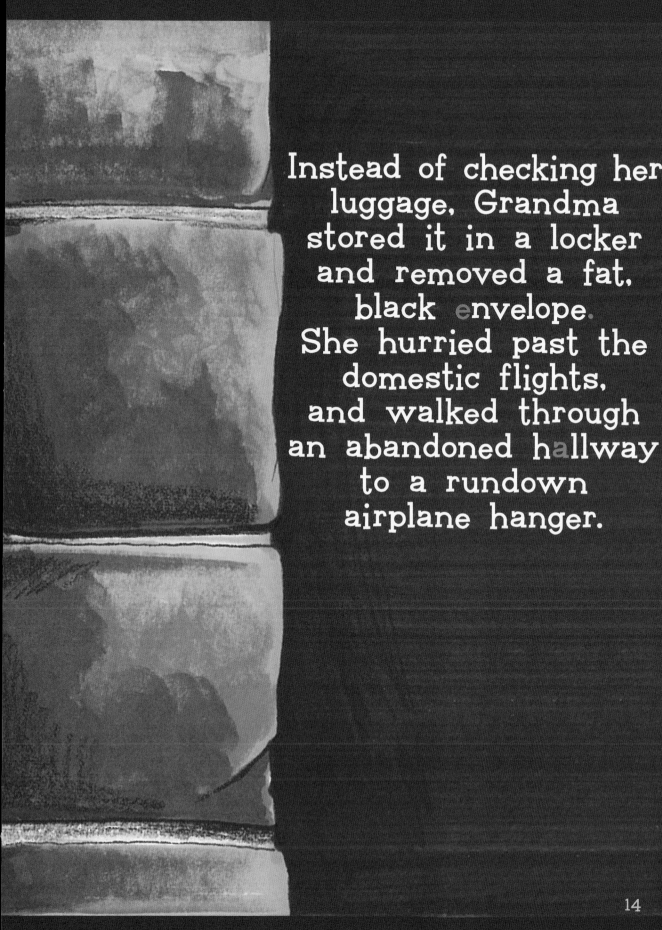

Instead of checking her luggage, Grandma stored it in a locker and removed a fat, black envelope. She hurried past the domestic flights, and walked through an abandoned hallway to a rundown airplane hanger.

A small plane and two soldiers
wearing army fatigues were
waiting for her. I snuck onto
the plane and hid under the seat.

"Agent Jean, everything is
in place to rescue the hostage,"
one soldier told her. "Thank you,
Sergeant." Grandma answered,
as she put on a long grey wig,
sunglasses and a tattered shawl.
We took off into the morning sun.

And I thought Grandma
had taken up hiking!

The plane landed. Five secret agents stood at attention. "Buenos tardes, señora," said one of the agents. "Buenos tardes," Grandma answered in a thick, Mexican accent. Mexico? I almost said out loud. Or maybe we flew all the way to Guatemala. I followed her.

We entered a bustling marketplace and I nearly lost her, because she blended in with everyone so well. I was also distracted by these cool stuffed donkeys, piled high in a vendor's booth.

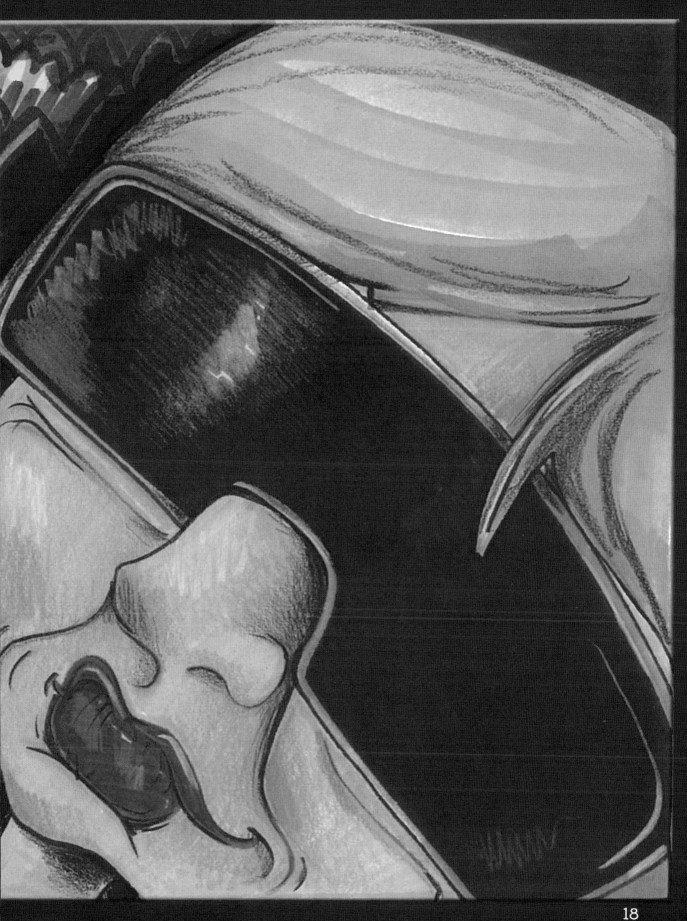

Finally, we came to a fortress
surrounded by guards.
I hid in the bushes and
watched. Grandma slowly
shuffled up to them.

"Can you spare a hot meal
for a poor blind woman?"
she wept. The guards
let her in without a thought.

Shouts followed.
In minutes she ran out
with the newly freed hostage
so fast I barely kept up.
"Code name Grambo.
We need an extraction team
ASAP!" She shouted
into her radio.

A helicopter appeared.
In the chaos, no one saw me
scramble onboard and hide
under a pile of uniforms.
My mind reeled.
Grandma is a SPY! A real SPY!
The helicopter flew us home.

Trailing behind her, I wound my way back to the domestic terminal. Grandma removed her luggage from the locker and stuffed in her disguise. She called my dad to pick her up. "I'm not feeling too well so I've decided to come home."

When my dad arrived,
I snuck into the backseat,
under the blanket.
When they were safely
inside our house and I couldn't
hold it in anymore, I burst in
screaming, "Grandma is a spy! She
works for the government..."

"Hi, Ryan. How was
Frankie's?" Dad asked.

"Did you hear what I said?!?
GRANDMA IS A SPY!"

Grandma kneeled next to me.
"Don't be silly, Ryan. You have
an amazing imagination, though.
Me? A spy?"

She seemed like just a
normal grandma. I wondered
if I'd dreamt it all.

"It was a short trip, but
I didn't forget your souvenir."
Grandma handed me the
stuffed donkey from the
marketplace and winked.

"Thanks Grambo!" I grinned at her.

Her secret was safe with me.
Besides, my mom and dad
would never believe me.

You may think you know your
grandma, but don't sell her short.
Because I found out
my Grandma can do anything!

the end

GRAMBO

The author:

Beth Navarro writes in Sierra Madre, California and fully believes grandmas rock. Please visit her website at www.bethnavarro.com.

The illustrator:

Betsy Hamilton lives and works in Illinois, where she spends as much time as possible drawing, painting and illustrating parachuting grannies.

Printed in Great Britain
by Amazon

86538143R00020